Granny Gomez & JIGSAW

For my mom
—D. U.

For Dad and the clubhouses he built
—S. M.

Reinforced binding
FIRST EDITION
1 3 5 7 9 10 8 6 4 2
Printed in Singapore

Library of Congress Cataloging-in-Publication Data on file.
ISBN 978-0-7868-5216-1

Visit www.hyperionbooksforchildren.com

Granny Gomez & JIGSAW

written by
DEBORAH UNDERWOOD

illustrated by
SCOTT MAGOON

Disney • Hyperion Books • New York

GRANNY GOMEZ lived in
a big old house in the country.

Granny liked her big house. It had
lots of room for her potted plants,
her drums, her mountain-climbing
gear, and her jigsaw puzzles.

But sometimes Granny was lonely.

"Maybe I will get a cat," she said to her petunias.

The petunias didn't say anything.

They never did.

"Maybe I will get a dog,"
she said to her pot of tulips.

The tulips didn't say anything either.

One day Granny's friend William came by for tea.
Granny told him about her plan to get a cat or a dog.
"Cats and dogs are nice, but they are not very special,"
William said. "You need a special pet."

"Like what?" Granny asked.

"I have an idea," said William.

The next day, Granny's doorbell rang.
DING-DONG!
There was a basket on her porch.
A blanket covered the basket.

The blanket moved.

"Goodness!" Granny said. "I wonder if it's a baby!"
She peeked under the blanket.

It *was* a baby.

Granny marched over to William's house.

"Pigs belong in barns, not houses," said Granny.

"You will have to take this little pig back."

William sighed. "All right, but I will have to take it back to Farmer Brown. He raises pigs for bacon."

"BACON? You mean this little pig will be somebody's breakfast?" Granny asked.

Granny looked at the pig's little pink nose. She looked at the pig's little pink ears. She looked at the pig's little pink tummy. The pig looked back at her with soft brown eyes. Granny made up her mind.

"No one is eating

THIS PIG!"

Granny took the pig home.

She carried him up the back stairs.
(Pigs are not very good with stairs.)

The pig was good company for Granny.

They both liked
cooking shows.

They both liked watermelon.

And they both liked jigsaw puzzles.
Whenever a piece fell off the table,
the pig scooted it over to Granny's feet.
"I think I will name you
JIGSAW,"
said Granny.

Having a pig in the house was not always easy.
And as Jigsaw got bigger, Granny's problems got bigger too.

A little pig
couldn't bite
Granny's skis in two.

But a big pig could.

A little pig couldn't
get stuck in Granny's
kitchen cupboard.

But a big pig could.

A little pig couldn't poke his head
through Granny's bass drum.
But a big pig could.

Each day, Granny carried Jigsaw down the stairs so they could walk in the park. Then she carried Jigsaw up the stairs so they could go inside and drink lemonade.

"My goodness," said Granny one day.

"You are getting big, Jigsaw."

"My goodness," panted Granny the next week.

"You are getting even bigger."

"My . . . goodness," gasped
Granny the next week.
"You are getting . . ."

CRASH!

Granny and Jigsaw fell through the stairs.
Granny looked at Jigsaw.
Jigsaw looked at Granny.
"I think it's time to build you
a nice barn," Granny said.

Granny drove her truck to Mrs. Green's hardware
store. Jigsaw rode in the front seat.

Granny bought lots of wood, lots of nails, and
BARN-BUILDING FOR BEGINNERS.

Granny piled the wood in her
yard and got right to work.

William helped.

Jigsaw helped too.

He ate sandwiches with Granny when she stopped for lunch.

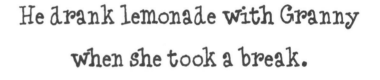

He drank lemonade with Granny when she took a break.

He ate cookies with Granny when she was done for the day.

Jigsaw helped so much that he got even bigger. Granny put a kitchen in the barn so Jigsaw could have snacks. She put shelves in the barn for puzzles.

She put a TV in the barn so Jigsaw could watch cooking shows. Finally the barn was finished. It was as nice as Granny's house.

Jigsaw snuggled into a pile of straw. He waited
for Granny to snuggle into a pile of straw too.

But she didn't.

"Now we each have a
place to live," Granny said.

Jigsaw blinked.

"Good night, Jigsaw.
I will see you tomorrow."

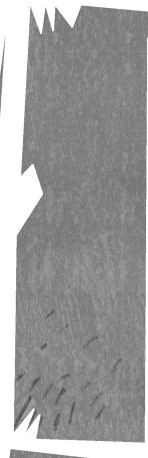

Granny went outside. Jigsaw followed her.

"No, Jigsaw," she said. "You stay here."

Jigsaw walked slowly back to the barn.

Granny walked slowly back to the house.

She had been very busy building the barn. She hadn't realized how much she would miss Jigsaw.

Until now.

Granny went inside. The house felt empty. She did a jigsaw puzzle. When a piece fell on the floor, no one scooted it back to her. She ate watermelon, but it didn't taste right. She watched BAILEY BAKES CRAZY CAKES, but it was no fun without Jigsaw.

Granny
looked out
at the barn.
She thought and thought.

Then she had an idea.

She packed her suitcase.

She tucked her camping bed under her arm.

She picked up her favorite chair.

Then she went out to the barn.

Jigsaw was waiting for her.